A Thorny P

Volume 07

Georg Ebers

(Translator: Clara Bell)

Alpha Editions

This edition published in 2023

ISBN : 9789357947800

Design and Setting By
Alpha Editions
www.alphaedis.com
Email - info@alphaedis.com

Contents

VOLUME 7.

CHAPTER XXI.

The high-priest of Serapis presided over the sacrifices to be offered this morning. Caesar had given beasts in abundance to do honor to the god; still, the priest had gone but ill-disposed to fulfill his part; for the imperial command that the citizens' houses should be filled with the troops, who were also authorized to make unheard-of demands on their hosts, had roused his ire against the tyrant, who, in the morning, after his bath, had appeared to him unhappy indeed, but at the same time a gifted and conscientious ruler, capable of the highest and grandest enterprise.

Melissa, in obedience to the lady Euryale, had taken an hour's rest, and then refreshed herself by bathing. She now was breakfasting with her venerated friend, and Philostratus had joined them. He was able to tell them that a swift State galley was already on its way to overtake and release her father and brother; and when he saw how glad she was to hear it, how beautiful, fresh, and pure she was, he thought to himself with anxiety that it would be a wonder if the imperial slave to his own passions should not desire to possess this lovely creature.

Euryale also feared this, and Melissa realized what filled them with anxiety; yet she by no means shared the feeling, and the happy confidence with which she tried to comfort her old friends, at the same time pacified and alarmed them. It seemed to her quite foolish and vain to suppose that the emperor, the mighty ruler of the world, should fall in love with her, the humble, obscure gem-cutter's child, who aspired to one suitor alone. It was merely as a patient wishes for the physician, she assured herself, that the emperor wished for her presence—Philostratus had understood that. During the night she had certainly been seized with great fears, but, as she now thought, without any cause. What she really had to dread was that she might be falsely judged by his followers; still, she cared nothing about all these Romans. However, she would beg Euryale to see Diodoros, and to tell him what forced her to obey the emperor's summons, if he should send for her. It was highly probable that the sick man had been informed of her interview with Caracalla, and, as her betrothed, he must be told how she felt toward Caesar; for this was his right, and jealous agitation might injure him.

Her face so expressed the hope and confidence of a pure heart that when, after a little time, she withdrew, Euryale said to the philosopher:

"We must not alarm her more! Her trustful innocence perhaps may protect her better than anxious precautions."

And Philostratus agreed, and assured her that in any case he expected good results for Melissa, for she was one of those who were the elect of the gods and whom they chose to be their instruments. And then he related what wonderful influence she had over Caesar's sufferings, and praised her with his usual enthusiastic warmth.

When Melissa returned, Philostratus had left the matron. She was again alone with Euryale, who reminded her of the lesson conveyed in the Christian words that she had explained to her yesterday. Every deed, every thought, had some influence on the way in which the fulfillment of time would come for each one; and when the hour of death was over, no regrets, repentance, or efforts could then alter the past. A single moment, as her own young experience had taught her, was often sufficient to brand the name of an estimable man. Till now, her way through life had led along level paths, through meadows and gardens, and others had kept their eyes open for her; now she was drawing near to the edge of a precipice, and at every turning, even at the smallest step, she must never forget the threatening danger. The best will and the greatest prudence could not save her if she did not trust to a higher guidance; and then she asked the girl to whom she raised her heart when she prayed; and Melissa named Isis and other gods, and lastly the manes of her dead mother.

During this confession, old Adventus appeared, to summon the girl to his sovereign. Melissa promised to follow him immediately; and, when the old man had gone, the matron said:

"Few here pray to the same gods, and he whose worship my husband leads is not mine. I, with several others, know that there is a Father in heaven who loves us men, his creatures, and guards us as his children. You do not yet know him, and therefore you can not hope for anything from him; but if you will follow the advice of a friend, who was also once young, think in the future that your right hand is held firmly by the invisible, beloved hand of your mother. Persuade yourself that she is by you, and take care that every word, yes, every glance, meets with her approval. Then she will be there, and will protect you whenever you require her aid."

Melissa sank on the breast of her kind friend, embracing her as closely and kissing her as sincerely as if she had been the beloved mother to whose care Euryale had commended her,

The counsels of this true friend agreed with those of her own heart, and so they must be right. When at last they had to part, Euryale wished to send for one of the gentlemen of the court, whom she knew, that he might escort her through the troops of Caesar's attendants and friends who were waiting, and of the visitors and petitioners; but Melissa felt so happy and so well protected by Adventus, that she followed him without further delay. In fact, the old man had a friendly feeling for her, since she had covered his feet so carefully the day before; she knew it by the tone of his voice and by the troubled look in his dim eyes.

Even now she did not believe in the dangers at which her friends trembled for her, and she walked calmly across the lofty marble halls, the anteroom, and the other vast rooms of the imperial dwelling. The attendants accompanied her respectfully from door to door, in obedience to the emperor's commands, and she went on with a firm step, looking straight in front of her, without noticing the inquisitive, approving, or scornful glances which were aimed at her.

In the first rooms she needed an escort, for they were crowded with Romans and Alexandrians who were waiting for a sign from Caesar to appeal for his pardon or his verdict, or perhaps only wishing to see his countenance. The emperor's "friends" sat at breakfast, of which Caracalla did not partake. The generals, and the members of his court not immediately attached to his person, stood together in the various rooms, while the principal people of Alexandria—several senators and rich and important citizens of the town— as well as the envoys of the Egyptian provinces, in magnificent garments and rich gold ornaments, held aloof from the Romans, and waited in groups for the call of the usher.

Melissa saw no one, nor did she observe the costly woven hangings on the walls, the friezes decorated with rare works of art and high reliefs, nor the mosaic floors over which she passed. She did not notice the hum and murmur of the numerous voices which surrounded her; nor could she indeed have understood a single coherent sentence; for, excepting the ushers and the emperor's immediate attendants, at the reception-hour no one was allowed to raise his voice. Expectancy and servility seemed here to stifle every lively impulse; and when, now and then, the loud call of one of the ushers rang above the murmur, one of those who were waiting spontaneously bowed low, or another started up, as if ready to obey any command. The sensation, shared by many, of waiting in the vicinity of a high, almost godlike power, in whose hands lay their well-being or misery, gave rise to a sense of solemnity. Every movement was subdued; anxious, nay, fearful expectation was written on many faces, and on others impatience and disappointment. After a little while it was whispered from ear to ear that the emperor would only grant a few more audiences; and how many had already waited in vain yesterday, for hours, in the same place!

Without delay Melissa went on till she had reached the heavy curtain which, as she already knew, shut off Caesar's inner apartments.

The usher obligingly drew it back, even before she had mentioned her name, and while a deputation of the town senators, who had been received by Caracalla, passed out, she was followed by Alexandrian citizens, the chiefs of great merchant-houses, whose request for an audience he had sanctioned. They were for the most part elderly men, and Melissa recognized among them Seleukus, Berenike's husband.

Melissa bowed to him, but he did not notice her, and passed by without a word. Perhaps he was considering the enormous sum to be expended on the show at night which he, with a few friends, intended to arrange at the circus in Caesar's honor.

All was quite still in the large hall which separated the emperor's reception-room from the anteroom. Melissa observed only two soldiers, who were looking out of window, and whose bodies were shaking as though they were convulsed with profound merriment.

It happened that she had to wait here some time; for the usher begged her to have patience until the merchants' audience was over. They were the last who would be received that day. He invited her to rest on the couch on which was spread a bright giraffe's skin, but she preferred to walk up and down, for her heart was beating violently. And while the usher vanished from the room, one of the warriors turned his head to look about him, and directly he caught sight of Melissa he gave his comrade a push, and said to him, loud enough for Melissa to hear:

"A wonder! Apollonaris, by Eros and all the Erotes, a precious wonder!"

The next moment they both stepped back from the window and stared at the girl, who stood blushing and embarrassed, and gazed at the floor when she found with whom she had been left alone.

They were two tribunes of the praetorians, but, notwithstanding their high grade, they were only young men of about twenty. Twin brothers of the honorable house of the Aurelia, they had entered the army as centurions, but had soon been placed at the head of a thousand men, and appointed tribunes in Caesar's body-guard. They resembled one another exactly; and this likeness, which procured them much amusement, they greatly enhanced by arranging their coal-black beards and hair in exactly the same way, and by dressing alike down to the rings on their fingers. One was called Apollonaris, the other Nemesianus Aurelius. They were of the same height, and equally well grown, and no one could say which had the finest black eyes, which mouth the haughtiest smile, or to which of them the thick short beard and the artistically shaved spot between the under lip and chin was most becoming. The beautifully embossed ornaments on their breast-plates and shirts of mail, and on the belt of the short sword, showed that they grudged no expense; in fact, they thought only of enjoyment, and it was merely for the honor of it that they were serving for a few years in the imperial guard. By and by they would rest, after all the hardships of the campaign, in their palace at Rome, or in the villas on the various estates that they had inherited from their father and mother, and then, for a change, hold honorary positions in the public service. Their friends knew that they also contemplated being married on the same day, when the game of war should be a thing of the past.

In the mean time they desired nothing in the world but honor and pleasure; and such pleasure as well-bred, healthy, and genial youths, with amiability, strength, and money to spend, can always command, they enjoyed to the full, without carrying it to reckless extravagance. Two merrier, happier, more popular comrades probably did not exist in the whole army. They did their duty in the field bravely; during peace, and in a town like Alexandria, they appeared, on the contrary, like mere effeminate men of fashion. At least, they spent a large part of their time in having their black hair crimped; they gave ridiculous sums to have it anointed with the most delicate perfumes; and it was difficult to imagine how effectively their carefully kept hands could draw a sword, and, if necessary, handle the hatchet or spade.

To-day Nemesianus was in the emperor's anteroom by command, and Apollonaris, of his own freewill, had taken the place of another tribune, that he might bear his brother company. They had caroused through half the night, and had begun the new day by a visit to the flower market, for love of the pretty saleswomen. Each had a half-opened rose stuck in between his cuirass and shirt of mail on the left breast, plucked, as the charming Daphnion had assured them, from a bush which had been introduced from Persia only the year before. The brothers, at any rate, had never seen any like them.

While they were looking out of the window they had passed the time by examining every girl or woman who went by, intending to fling one rose at the first whose perfect beauty should claim it, and the other flower at the second; but during the half-hour none had appeared who was worthy of such a gift. All the beauties in Alexandria were walking in the streets in the cool hour before sunset, and really there was no lack of handsome girls. The brothers had even heard that Caesar, who seemed to have renounced the pleasures of love, had yielded to the charms of a lovely Greek.

Directly they saw Melissa they were convinced that they had met the beautiful plaything of the imperial fancy, and each with the same action offered her his rose, as if moved by the same invisible power.

Apollonaris, who had come into the world a little sooner than his brother, and who, by right of birth, had therefore a more audacious manner, stepped boldly up to Melissa and presented his, while Nemesianus at the same instant bowed to her, and begged her to give his the preference.

Though their speeches were flattering and well-worded, Melissa repulsed them by remarking sharply that she did not want their flowers.

"We can easily believe that," answered Apollonaris, "for are you not yourself a lovely, blooming rose?"

"Vain flattery," replied Melissa; "and I certainly do not bloom for you."

"That is both cruel and unjust," sighed Nemesianus, "for that which you refuse to us poor fellows you grant to another, who can obtain everything that other mortals yearn for."

"But we," interrupted his brother, "are modest, nay, and pious warriors. We had intended offering up these roses to Aphrodite, but lo! the goddess has met us in person."

"Her image at any rate," added the other.

"And you should thank the foam-born goddess," continued Apollonaris; "for she has lent you, in spite of the danger of seeing herself eclipsed, her own divine charms. Do you think she will be displeased if we withdraw the flowers and offer them to you?"

"I think nothing," answered Melissa, "excepting that your honeyed remarks annoy me. Do what you like with your roses, I will not accept them."

"How dare you," asked Apollonaris, approaching her—"you, to whom the mother of love has given such wonderfully fresh lips—misuse them by refusing so sternly the humble petition of her faithful worshipers? If you would not have Aphrodite enraged with you, hasten to atone for this transgression. One kiss, my beauty, for her votary, and she will forgive you."

Here Apollonaris stretched out his hand toward the girl to draw her to him, but she motioned him back indignantly, declaring that it would be reprehensible and cowardly in a soldier to use violence toward a modest maid.

At this the two brothers laughed heartily, and Nemesianus exclaimed, "You do not belong to the Temple of Vesta, most lovely of roses, and yet you are well protected by such sharp thorns that it requires a great deal of courage to venture to attack you."

"More," added Apollonaris, "than to storm a fortress. But what camp or stronghold contains booty so well worth capturing?"

Thereupon he threw his arm round Melissa and drew her to him.

Neither he nor his brother had ever conducted themselves badly towards an honorable woman; and if Melissa had been but the daughter of a simple craftsman, her reproachful remarks would have sufficed to keep them at a distance. But such immunity was not to be granted to the emperor's sweetheart, who could so audaciously reject two brothers accustomed to easy conquests; her demure severity could hardly be meant seriously. Apollonaris therefore took no notice of her violent resistance, but held her hands forcibly, and, though he could not succeed in kissing her for her struggling, he pressed his lips to her cheek, while she endeavored to free herself and pushed him off, breathless with real indignation.

'Till now, the brothers had taken the matter as a joke; but when Apollonaris seized the girl again, and she, beside herself with fear, cried for help, he at once set her free.

It was too late; for the curtains of the audience-room were already withdrawn, and Caracalla approached. His countenance was red and distorted; he trembled with rage, and his angry glance fell like a flash of lightning on the luckless brothers. Close by his side was the prefect Macrinus, who feared lest he should be attacked by a fresh fit; and Melissa shared his fears, as Caracalla cried to Apollonaris in an angry voice, "Scoundrel that you are, you shall repent of this!"

Still, Aurelius had, by various wanton jokes, incurred the emperor's wrath before now, and he was accustomed to disarm it by some insinuating confession, so he answered him with a roguish smile, while raising his eyes to him humbly:

"Forgive me, great Caesar! Our poor strength, as you well know, is easily defeated in conflicts against overpowering beauty. Dainties are sweet, not only for children. Long ago Mars was drawn to Venus; and if I—"

He had spoken these words in Latin, which Melissa did not understand; but the color left the emperor's face, and, pale with excitement, he stammered out laboriously:

"You have—you have dared—"

"For this rose," began the youth again, "I begged a hasty kiss from the beauty, which certainly blooms for all, and she—" He raised his hands and eyes imploringly to the despot; but Caracalla had already snatched Macrinus's sword from its sheath, and before Aurelius could defend himself he was struck first on the head with the flat of the blade, and then received a series of sharp cuts on his brow and face.

Streaming with blood from the gaping wounds which the victim, trembling with fear and rage, covered with his hands, he surrendered himself to the care of his startled brother, while Caesar overwhelmed them both with a flood of furious reproaches.

When Nemesianus began to bind up his wounded brother's head with a handkerchief handed to him by Melissa, and Caracalla saw the gaping wounds he had inflicted, he became quieter, and said:

"I think those lips will not try to steal kisses again for some time from honorable maidens. You and Nemesianus have forfeited your lives; how ever, the beseeching look of those all-powerful eves has saved you—you are spared. Take your brother away, Nemesianus. You are not to leave your quarters until further orders."

With this he turned his back on the twins, but on the threshold he again addressed them and said:

"You were mistaken about this maiden. She is not less pure and noble than your own sister."

The merchants were dismissed from the tablinum more hastily than was due to the importance of their business, in which, until this interruption, the sovereign had shown a sympathetic interest and intelligence which surprised them; and they left Caesar's presence disappointed, but with the promise that they should be received again in the evening.

As soon as they had retired, Caracalla threw himself again on the couch.

The bath had done him good. Still somewhat exhausted, though his head was clear, he would not be hindered from receiving the deputation for which he had important matters to decide; but this fresh attack of rage revenged itself by a painful headache. Pale, and with slightly quivering limbs, he dismissed the prefect and his other friends, and desired Epagathos to call Melissa.

He needed rest, and again the girl's little hand, which had yesterday done him good, proved its healing power. The throbbing in his head yielded to her gentle touch, and by degrees exhaustion gave way to the comfortable languor of convalesence.

To-day, as yesterday, he expressed his thanks to Melissa, but he found her changed. She looked timidly and anxiously down into her lap excepting when she replied to a direct question; and yet he had done everything to please her. Her relations would soon be free and in Alexandria once more, and Zminis was in prison, chained hand and foot. This he told her; and, though she was glad, it was not enough to restore the calm cheerfulness he had loved to see in her.

He urged her, with warm insistence, to tell him what it was that weighed on her, and at last, with eyes full of tears, she forced herself to say:

"You yourself have seen what they take me for."

"And you have seen," he quickly replied, "how I punish those who forget the respect they owe to you."

"But you are so dreadful in your wrath!" The words broke from her lips. "Where others blame, you can destroy; and you do it, too, when passion carries you away. I am bound to obey your call, and here I am. But I fancy myself like the little dog—you may see him any day—which in the beast-garden of the Panaeum, shares a cage with a royal tiger. The huge brute puts up with a great deal from his small companion, but woe betide the dog if the tiger once pats him with his heavy, murderous paw—and he might, out of sheer forgetfulness!"

"But this hand," Caesar broke in, raising his delicate hand covered with rings, "will never forget, any more than my heart, how much it owes to you."

"Until I, in some unforeseen way—perhaps quite unconsciously—excite your anger," sighed Melissa. "Then you will be carried away by passion, and I shall share the common fate."

Caracalla was about to reply indignantly, but just then Adventus entered the room, announcing the chief astrologer of the Temple of Serapis. Caracalla refused to receive him just then, but he anxiously asked whether he had any signs to report. The reply was in the affirmative, and in a few minutes Caesar had in his hand a wax tablet covered with words and figures. He studied it eagerly, and his countenance cleared; still holding the tablets, he exclaimed to Melissa:

"You, daughter of Heron, have nothing to fear from me, you of all the world! In some quiet hour I will explain to you how my planet yearns to yours, and yours—that is, yourself—to mine. The gods have created us for each other, child; I am already under your influence, but your heart still hesitates, and I know why; it is because you distrust me."

Melissa raised her large eyes to his face in astonishment, and he went on, pensively:

"The past must stand; it is like a scar which no water will wash out. What have you not heard of my past? What did they feel, in their self- conscious virtue, when they talked of my crimes? Did it ever occur to any one, I wonder, that with the purple I assumed the sword, to protect my empire and throne? And when I have used the blade, how eagerly have fingers pointed at me, how gladly slanderous tongues have wagged! Who has ever thought of asking what compulsion led me to shed blood, or how much it cost me to do it? You, fair child—and the stars confirm it—you were sent by fate to share the burden that oppresses me, and to you I will ease my heart, to you I will confide all, unasked, because my heart prompts me to do so. But first you must tell me with what tales they taught you to hate the man to whom, as you yourself confessed, you nevertheless felt drawn."

At this Melissa raised her hands in entreaty and remonstrance, and Caesar went on:

"I will spare you the pains. They say that I am ever athirst for fresh bloodshed if only some one is rash enough to suggest it to me. You were told that Caesar murdered his brother Geta, with many more who did but speak his victim's name. My father-in-law, and his daughter Plautilla, my wife, were, it is said, the victims of my fury. I killed Papinian, the lawyer and prefect, and Cilo— whom you saw yesterday—nearly shared the same fate. What did they conceal? Nothing. Your nod confesses it— well, and why should they, since speaking ill of others is their greatest delight? It is all true, and I should never think of denying it. But did it ever occur to you, or did any one ever suggest to you, to inquire how it came to pass that I perpetrated such horrors; I— who was brought up in the fear of the gods and the law, like you and other people?"

"No, my lord, never," replied Melissa, in distress. "But I beg you, I beseech you, say no more about such dreadful things. I know full well that you are not wicked; that you are much better than people think."

"And for that very reason," cried Caesar, whose cheeks were flushed with pleasure in the hard task he had set himself, "you must hear me. I am Caesar. There is no judge over me; I need give account to none for my actions. Nor do I. Who, besides yourself, is more to me than the flies on that cup?"

"And your conscience?" she timidly put in.

"It raises hideous questions from time to time," he replied, gloomily. "It can be obtrusive, but we can teach ourselves not to answer—besides, what you call conscience knows the motives for every action, and, remembering them, judges leniently. You, child, should do the same; for you—"

"O my lord, what can my poor judgment matter?" Melissa panted out; but Caracalla exclaimed, as if the question pained him:

"Must I explain all that? The stars, as you know, proclaim to you, as to me, that a higher power has joined us as light and warmth are joined. Have you forgotten how we both felt only yesterday? Or am I mistaken? Has not Roxana's soul entered into that divinely lovely form because it longed for its lost companion spirit?"

He spoke vehemently, with a quivering of his eyelids; but feeling her hand tremble in his own, he collected himself, and went on in a lower tone, but with urgent emphasis:

"I will let you glance into this bosom, closed to every other eye; for my desolate heart is inspired by you to fresh energy and life; I am as grateful to you as a drowning man to his deliverer. I shall suffocate and die if I repress the impulse to open my heart to you!"

What change was this that had come over this mysterious being? Melissa felt as though she was gazing on the face of a stranger, for, though his eyelids still quivered, his eyes were bright with ecstatic fire and his features looked more youthful. On that noble brow the laurel wreath he wore looked well. Also, as she now observed, he was magnificently attired; he wore a close-fitting tunic, or breast-plate made of thick woolen stuff, and over it a purple mantle, while from his bare throat hung a precious medallion, shield-shaped, and set in gold and gems, the center formed by a large head of Medusa, with beautiful though terrible features. The lion-heads of gold attached to each corner of the short cloak he wore over the sham coat of mail, were exquisite works of art, and sandals embroidered with gold and gems covered his feet and ankles. He was dressed to-day like the heir of a lordly house, anxious to charm; nay, indeed, like an emperor, as he was; and with what care had his body- slave arranged his thin curls!

He passed his hand over his brow and cast a glance at a silver mirror on the low table at the head of his couch. When he turned to her again his amorous eyes met Melissa's.

She looked down in startled alarm. Was it for her sake that Caesar had thus decked himself and looked in the mirror? It seemed scarcely possible, and yet it flattered and pleased her. But in the next instant she longed more fervently than she ever had before for a magic charm by which she might vanish and be borne far, far away from this dreadful man. In fancy she saw the vessel which the lady Berenike had in readiness. She would, she must fly hence, even if it should part her for a time from Diodoros.

Did Caracalla read her thought? Nay, he could not see through her; so she endured his gaze, tempting him to speak; and his heart beat high with hope as he fancied he saw that she was beginning to be affected by his intense agitation. At this moment he felt convinced, as he often had been, that the most atrocious of his crimes had been necessary and inevitable. There was something grand and vast in his deeds of blood, and that—for he flattered himself he knew the female heart—must win her admiration, besides the awe and love she already felt.

During the night, at his waking, and in his bath, he had felt that she was as necessary to him as the breath of life and hope. What he experienced was love as the poets had sung it. How often had he laughed it to scorn, and boasted that he was armed against the arrows of Eros! Now, for the first time, he was aware of the anxious rapture, the ardent longing of which he had read in so many songs. There stood the object of his passion. She must hear him, must be his—not by compulsion, not by imperial command, but of the free impulse of her heart.

His confession would help to this end.

With a swift gesture, as if to throw off the last trace of fatigue, he sat up and began in a firm voice, with a light in his eyes:

"Yes, I killed my brother Geta. You shudder. And yet, if at this day, when I know all the results of the deed, the state of affairs were the same as then, I would do it again! That shocks you. But only listen, and then you will say with me that it was Fate which compelled me to act so, and not otherwise."

He paused, and then mistaking the anxiety which was visible in Melissa's face for sympathetic attention, he began his story, confident of her interest:

"When I was born, my father had not yet assumed the purple, but he already aimed at the sovereignty. Augury had promised it to him; my mother knew this, and shared his ambition. While I was still at my nurse's breast he was made consul; four years later he seized the throne. Pertinax was killed, the wretched Didius Julianus bought the empire, and this brought my father to Rome from Pannonia. Meanwhile he had sent us children, my brother Geta and me, away from the city; nor was it till he had quelled the last resistance on the Tiber that he recalled us.

"I was then but a child of five, and yet one day of that time I remember vividly. My father was going through Rome in solemn procession. His first object was to do due honor to the corpse of Pertinax. Rich hangings floated from every window and balcony in the city. Garlands of flowers and laurel wreaths adorned the houses, and pleasant odors were wafted to us as we went. The jubilation of the people was mixed with the trumpet-call of the soldiers; handkerchiefs were waved and acclamations rang out. This was in honor of my father, and of me also, the future Caesar. My little heart was almost bursting with pride; it seemed to me that I had grown several heads taller, not only than other boys, but than the people that surrounded me.

"When the funeral procession began, my mother wished me to go with her into the arcade where seats had been placed for the ladies to view, but I refused to follow her. My father became angry. But when he heard me declare that I was a man and the future Emperor, that I would rather see nothing than show myself to the people among the women, he smiled. He ordered Cilo, who was then the prefect of Rome, to lead me to the seats of the past consuls and the old senators. I was delighted at this; but when he allowed my younger brother Geta to follow me, my pleasure was entirely spoiled."

"And you were then five years old?" asked Melissa, astonished.

"That surprises you!" smiled Caracalla. "But I had already traveled through half the empire, and had experienced more than other boys of twice my age. I was, at any rate, still child enough to forget everything else in the brilliant spectacle that unfolded before my eyes. I remember to this day the colored wax statue which represented Pertinax so exactly that it might have been himself risen from the grave. And the procession! It seemed to have no end; one new thing followed another. All walked past in mourning robes, even the choir of singing boys and men. Cilo explained to me who had made the statues of the Romans who had served their country, who the artists and scholars were, whose statues and busts were carried by. Then came bronze groups of the people of every nation in the empire, in their costumes. Cilo told me what they were called, and where they lived; he then added that one day they would all belong to me; that I must learn the art of fighting, in case they resisted me, and should require suppressing. Also, when they carried the flags of the guilds past, when the horse and foot soldiers, the race- horses from the circus and several other things came by, he continued to explain them. I only remember it now because it made me so happy. The old man spoke to me alone; he regarded me alone as the future sovereign. He left Geta to eat the sweets which his aunts had given him, and when I too wanted some my brother refused to let me have any. Then Cilo stroked my hair, and said: 'leave him his toys. When you are a man you shall have the whole Roman Empire for your own, and all the nations I told you of.' Geta meanwhile had thought better of it, and pushed some of the sweetmeats toward me. I would not have them, and, when he tried to make me take them, I threw them into the road."

"And you remember all that?" said Melissa.

"More things than these are indelibly stamped on my mind from that day," said Caesar. "I can see before me now the pile on which Pertinax was to be burned. It was splendidly decorated, and on the top stood the gilt chariot in which he had loved to ride. Before the consuls fired the logs of Indian wood, my father led us to the image of Pertinax, that we might kiss it. He held me by the hand. Wherever we went, the senate and people hailed us with acclamations. My mother carried Geta in her arms. This delighted the populace. They shouted for her and my brother as enthusiastically as for us, and I recollect to this day how that went to my heart. He might have the sweets and welcome, but what the people had to offer was due only to my father and me, not to my brother. At that moment I first fully understood that Severus was the present and I the future Caesar. Geta had only to obey, like every one else.

"After kissing the image, I stood, still holding my father's hand, to watch the flames. I can see them now, crackling and writhing as they gained on the wood, licking it and fawning, as it were, till it caught and sent up a rush of sparks and fire. At last the whole pile was one huge blaze. Then, suddenly, out of the heart of the flames an eagle rose. The creature flapped its broad wings in the air, which was golden with sunshine and quivering with heat, soaring above the smoke and fire, this way and that. But it soon took flight, away from the furnace beneath. I shouted with delight, and cried to my father: 'Look at the bird! Where is he flying?' And he eagerly answered: 'Well done! If you desire to preserve the power I have conquered for you always undiminished, you must keep your eyes open. Let no sign pass unnoticed, no opportunity neglected.'

"He himself acted on this rule. To him obstacles existed only to be removed, and he taught me, too, to give myself neither peace nor rest, and not to spare the life of a foe.—That festival secured my father the suffrages of the Romans. Meanwhile Pescennius Niger rose up in the East with a large army and took the field against Severus. But my father was not the man to hesitate. Within a few months of the obsequies of Pertinax his opponent was a headless corpse.

"There was yet another obstacle to be removed. You have heard of Clodius Albinus. My father had adopted him and raised him to share his throne. But Severus could not divide the rule with any man.

"When I was nine years old I saw, after the battle of Lugdunum, the dead face of Albinus's head; it was set up in front of the Curia on a lance.

"I now was the second personage in the empire, next to my father; the first among the youth of the whole world, and the future emperor. When I was eleven the soldiers hailed me as Augustus; that was in the war against the Parthians, before Ktesiphon. But they did the same to Geta. This was like wormwood in the sweet draught; and if then—But what can a girl care about the state, and the fate of rulers and nations?"

"Yes, go on," said Melissa. "I see already what you are coming to. You disliked the idea of sharing your power with another."

"Nay," cried Caracalla, vehemently, "I not only disliked it, it was intolerable, impossible! What I want you to see is that I did not grudge my brother his share of my father's inheritance, like any petty trader. The world—that is the point—the world itself was too small for two of us. It was not I, but Fate, which had doomed Geta to die. I am certain of this, and so must you be. Yes, it was Fate. Fate prompted the child's little hand to attempt its brother's life. And that was long before my brain could form a thought or my baby-lips could stammer his hated name."

"Then you tried to kill your brother even in infancy?" asked Melissa, and her large eyes dilated with horror as she gazed at the terrible narrator. But Caracalla went on, in an apologetic tone:

"I was then but two years old. It was at Mediolanum, soon after Geta's birth. An egg was found in the court of the palace; a hen had laid it close to a pillar. It was of a purple hue-red all over like the imperial mantle, and this indicated that the newly born infant was destined to sovereignty. Great was the rejoicing. The purple marvel was shown even to me who could but just walk. I, like a naughty boy, flung it down; the shell cracked, and the contents poured out on the pavement. My mother saw it, and her exclamation, 'Wicked child, you have murdered your brother!' was often repeated to me in after-years. It never struck me as particularly motherly."

Here he paused, gazing meditatively into vacancy, and then asked the girl, who had listened intently:

"Were you never haunted by a word so that you could not be rid of it?"

"Oh, yes," cried Melissa; "a striking rhythm in a song, or a line of poetry—"

Caracalla nodded agreement, and went on more vehemently: "That is what I experienced at the words, 'You have murdered your brother!' I not only heard them now and then with my inward ear, but incessantly, like the dreary hum of the flies in my camp-tent, for hours at a time, by day and by night. No fanning could drive these away. The diabolical voice whispered loudest when Geta had done anything to vex me; or if things had been given him which I did not wish him to have. And how often that happened! For I—I was only Bassianus to my mother; but her youngest was her dear little Geta.

"So the years passed. We had, while still quite young, our own teams in the circus. One day, when we were driving for a wager-we were still boys, and I was ahead of the other lads—the horses of my chariot shied to one side. I was thrown some distance on the course. Geta saw this. He turned his horses to the right where I lay. He drove over his brother as he would over straw and apple-parings in the dust; and his wheel broke my thigh. Who knows what else it crushed in me? One thing is certain— from that date the most painful of my sufferings originated. And he, the mean scoundrel, had done it intentionally. He had sharp eyes. He knew how to guide his steeds. He had never driven his wheel over a hazel-nut in the sand of the arena against his will; and I was lying some distance from the driving course."

Caesar's eyelids blinked spasmodically as he uttered this accusation, and his very glance revealed the raging fire that was burning in his soul. Melissa's sad cry of:

"What terrible suspicion!" he answered with a short, scornful laugh and the furious assertion:

"Oh, there were friends enough who informed me what hope Geta had founded on this act of treachery. The disappointment made him irritable and listless, when Galenus had succeeded in curing me so far that I was able to throw away my Crutch; and my limp—at least so they tell me—is hardly perceptible."

"Not at all, most certainly not at all," Melissa sympathetically assured him. He, however, went on:

"Yet what I endured meanwhile!—and while I passed so many long weeks of pain and impatience on a couch, the words my mother had said about the brother whom I murdered rang constantly in my ears as though a reciter were engaged by day and night to reiterate them.

"But even this passed away. With the pain, which had spoiled many good hours for me, the quiet had brought me something more to the purpose-thoughts and plans. Yes, during those peaceful weeks the things my father and tutor had taught me became clear and real for the first time. I realized that I must become energetic if I meant ever to be a thorough sovereign. As soon as I could use my foot again I became an industrious and docile pupil under Cilo. From a child up to the time of this cruel experience, my youthful heart had clung to my nurse. She was a Christian from my father's African home—I knew she loved me best on earth. My mother knew of no higher destiny than that of being the Domna,—[Domna, lady or mistress, in corrupt Latin. Hence her name of Julia Domna] the lady of the soldiers, the mother of the camp, and the lady philosopher among the sages. What she gave me in the way of love was but copper alms. She threw golden solidi of love into Geta's lap in lavish abundance. And her sister and her nieces, who often lived with us, treated me exactly as she did. They were distantly civil, or they shunned me; but my brother was their spoiled plaything. I was as incapable as Geta was master of the art of stealing hearts; but in my childhood I needed none of them: for, if I wished for a kind word, a sweet kiss, or the love of a woman, my nurse's arms were open to me. Nor was she an ordinary woman. As the widow of a tribune who had fallen in my father's service, she had undertaken to attend on me. She loved me as no one else ever did. She was also the only person whom I would willingly obey. I came into the world full of wild instincts, but she knew how to tame them kindly. My aversion to my brother was the one thing she checked but feebly, for he was a thorn in her side too. I learned this when she, who was so gentle, explained to me, with asperity in her tone, that there was but one God in heaven, and on earth but one emperor, who should govern the world in his name. She also imparted these convictions to others, and this turned to her disadvantage. My mother parted us, and sent her back to her African home. She died soon after." He was silent, and gazed pensively into vacancy; soon, however, he collected his thoughts and said, lightly:

"Well, I became Cilo's diligent pupil."

"But," asked Melissa, "did you not say that at one time you attempted his life?"

"I did so," replied Caracalla darkly; "for a moment arrived when I cursed his teaching, and yet it was certainly wise and well meant. You see, child, all of you who go through life humbly and without power are trained to submit obediently to the will of Heaven. Cilo taught me to place my own power, and the greatness of the realm which it would be incumbent on me to reign over, above everything, even above the gods. It was impressed upon you and yours to hold the life of another sacred; to us, our duty as the sovereign transcends this law. Even the blood of a brother must flow if it is for the good of the state intrusted to us. My nurse had taught me that being good meant doing unto others as we would be done by; Cilo cried to me: 'Strike down, that you may not be struck down—away with mercy, if the welfare of the state is threatened!' And how many hands are raised against Rome, the universal empire, which I rule over! It needs a strong hand to keep its antagonistic parts together. Otherwise it would fall apart like a bundle of arrows when the string that bound them is broken. And I, even as a boy, had sworn to my father, by the Terminus stone in the Capitol, never to abandon a single inch of his ground without fighting for it. He, Severus, was the wisest of the rulers. Only the blind love for his second son, encouraged by the women, caused him to forget his moderation and prudence. My brother Geta was to reign together with me over the empire, which ought to have been mine alone as the first-born. Every year festivals were kept, with prayers and sacrifices, to the "love of the brothers." You have perhaps seen the coins, which show us hand in hand, and have on them the inscription, 'Eternal union'!

"I in union—I hand in hand with the man I most hated under the sun! It almost maddened me only to hear his voice. I would have liked best of all to spring at his throat when I saw him with his learned fellows squandering their time. Do you know what they did? They invented the names by which the voices of different animals were to be known. Once I snatched the pencil out of the hand of the freedman as he was writing the sentences, 'The horse neighs, the pig grunts, the goat bleats, the cow lows, the sheep baas.' 'He, himself,' I added, 'croaks like a hoarse jay.'

"That I should share the government with this miserable, faint-hearted, poisonous nobody could never be,—this enemy, who, when I said 'Yes,' cried 'No!' Who frustrated all my measures,—it was impossible! It would have caused the destruction of the state, as certainly as it was the unfairest and unwisest of the deeds of Severus, to place the younger brother as co-regent with the first-born, the rightful heir to the throne. I, whom my father had taught to watch for signs, was reminded every hour that this unbearable position must come to an end.

"After the death of Severus, we lived at first close to one another in separate parts of the same palace like two lions in a cage across which a partition has been erected, so that they may not reciprocally mangle each other.

"We used to meet at my mother's.

"That morning my mastiff had bitten Geta's wolfhound and killed him, and they had found a black liver in the beast he had sent for sacrifice. I had been informed of this. Destiny was on my side. This indolent inactivity must be brought to a close. I myself do not know how I felt as I mounted the steps to my mother's rooms. I only remember distinctly that a demon cried continually in my ear, 'You have murdered your brother!' Then I suddenly found myself face to face with him. It was in the empress's reception-room. And when I saw the hated flat-shaped head so close to me, when his beardless mouth with its thick underlip smiled at me so sweetly and at the same time so falsely, I felt as if I again heard the cry with which he had cheered on his horse. And I felt . . . I even felt the pain-as if he broke my thigh again with his wheel. And at the same time a fiend whispered in my ear: 'Destroy him, or he will kill you, and through him Rome will perish!'

"Then I seized my sword. In his odious, peevish voice he said something — I forget what nonsense—to me. Then it appeared to me as if all the sheep and goats over which he had squandered his time were bleating at me. The blood rushed to my head. The room spun round me in a circle. Black spots on a red ground danced before my eyes.

"And then—What flashed in my right hand was my own naked sword! I neither heard nor said anything further. Nor had I planned, nor ever thought of, what then occurred. . . . But suddenly I felt as if a mountain of oppressive lead had fallen from my breast. How easily I could breathe again! All that had just before turned round me in a mad, whirling dance stood still. The sun shone brightly in the large room; a shaft of light, showing dancing dust, fell on Geta. He sank on his knees close to me, with my sword in his breast. My mother made a fruitless effort to shield him. His blood trickled over her hand. I can still see every ring on those slender, white fingers. I also remember distinctly how, when I raised my sword against him, my mother rushed in between us to protect her favorite. The sharp blade, as she tried to seize it, accidentally grazed her hand—I know not how—only the skin was slightly cut. Yet what a scream she gave over the wound which the son had given his mother! Julia Maesa, her daughter Mammara, and the other women, rushed in. How they exaggerated! They made a river out of every drop of blood.

"So the dreadful deed was done; and yet, had I let the wretch live, I should have been a traitor to Rome, to myself, and to my father's life's work. That day, for the first time, I was ruler of the world. Those who accuse me of fratricide no doubt believe themselves to be right. But they certainly are not. I know better. You also know now with me that destiny, and not I, struck Geta out from among the living."

Here he sat for some time in breathless silence. Then he asked Melissa:

"You understand now how I came to shed my brother's blood?"

She started, and repeated gently after him: "Yes, I understand it."

Deep compassion filled her heart, and yet she felt she dare not sanction what she had heard and deplored. Torn by deep and conflicting feelings she threw back her head, brushed her hair off her face, and cried: "Let me go now; I can bear it no longer!"

"So soft-hearted?" asked he, and shook his head disapprovingly. "Life rages more wildly round the throne than in an artist's home. You will have to learn to swim through the roaring torrent with me. Believe me, even enormities can become quite commonplace. And, besides, why does it still shock you when you yourself know that it was indispensable?"

"I am only a weak girl, and I feel as if I had witnessed these fearful deeds, and had to bear the terrible blood-guiltiness with you!" broke from her lips.

"That is what you must and shall do! It is to that end that I have confided to you what no one else has ever heard from my mouth!" cried Caracalla, his eyes flashing more brightly. She felt as though this cry called her from her slumbers and revealed the precipice to which she had strayed in her sleepwalking.

When Caracalla had begun telling her of his youth, she had only listened with half an ear; for she could not forget Berenike's rescuing ship. But soon his confessions completely attracted her attention, and the lament of this powerful man on whom so many injuries and wrongs had fallen, who even in childhood had been deprived of the happiness of a mother's love, had touched her tender heart. That which was afterward told to her she had identified with her own humble life; she heard with a shudder that it was to the malice of his brother that this unhappy being owed the injury which, like a poisonous blight, had marred for him all the joys of existence, while she owed all that was loveliest and best in her young life to a brother's love.

The grounds on which Caracalla had based the assertion that destiny had compelled him to murder Geta appeared to her young and inexperienced mind as indisputable. He was only the pitiable victim of his birth and of a cruel fate. Besides, the humblest and most sober-minded can not resist the charm of majesty; and this hapless man, who had honored Melissa with his confidence, and who had assured her so earnestly that she was of such importance to him and could do so much for him, was the ruler of the universe.

She had also felt, after Caesar's confession, that she had a right to be proud, since he had thought her worthy to take an interest in the tragedy in the imperial palace, as if she had been a member of the court. In her lively imagination she had witnessed the ghastly act to which he—as she had certainly believed, even when she had replied to his question—had been forced by fate.

But the demand which had followed her answer now recurred to her. The picture of Diodoros, which had completely vanished from her thoughts while she had been listening, suddenly appeared to her, and, as she fancied, he looked at her reproachfully.

Had she, then, transgressed against her betrothed?

No, no, indeed she had not!

She loved him, and only him; and for that very reason, her upright judgment told her now, that it would be sinning against her lover to carry out Caracalla's wish, as if she had become his fellow-culprit, or certainly the advocate of the bloody outrage. She could think of no answer to his "That is what you must and shall do!" that would not awaken his wrath. Cautiously, and with sincere thanks for his confidence in her, she begged him once more to allow her to leave him, because she needed rest after such a shock to her mind. And it would also do him good to grant himself a short rest. But he assured her he knew that he could only rest when he had fulfilled his duty as a sovereign. His father had said, a few minutes before he drew his last breath:

"If there is anything more to be done, give it me to do," and he, the son, would do likewise.

"Moreover," he concluded, "it has done me good to bring to light that which I had for so long kept sealed within me. To gaze in your face at the same time was, perhaps, even better physic."

At this he rose and, seizing the startled girl by both hands, he cried:

"You, child, can satisfy the insatiable! The love which I offer you resembles a full bunch of grapes, and yet I am quite content if you will give me back but one berry."

At the very commencement, this declaration was drowned by a loud shout which rang through the room in waves of sound.

Caracalla started, but, before he could reach the window, old Adventus rushed in breathless; and he was followed, though in a more dignified manner, with a not less hasty step and every sign of excitement, by Macrinus, the prefect of the praetorians, with his handsome young son and a few of Caesar's friends.

"This is how I rest!" exclaimed Caracalla, bitterly, as he released Melissa's hand and turned inquiringly to the intruders.

The news had spread among the praetorians and the Macedonian legions, that the emperor, who, contrary to his custom, had not shown himself for two days, was seriously ill, and at the point of death. Feeling extremely anxious about one who had showered gold on them, and given them such a degree of freedom as no other imperator had ever allowed them, they had collected before the Serapeum and demanded to see Caesar. Caracalla's eyes lighted up at this information, and, excitedly pleased, he cried:

"They only are really faithful!"

He asked for his sword and helmet, and sent for the 'paludamentum', the general's cloak of purple, embroidered with gold, which he never otherwise wore except on the field. The soldiers should see that he intended leading in future battles.

While they waited, he conversed quietly with Macrinus and the others; when, however, the costly garment covered his shoulders, and when his favorite, Theocritus, who had known best how to support him during his illness, offered him an arm, he answered imperiously that he required no assistance.

"Nevertheless, you should, after so serious an attack—" the physician in ordinary ventured to exhort him; but he interrupted him scornfully, and, glancing toward Melissa, exclaimed:

"Those little hands there contain more healing power than yours and the great Galenus's put together."

Thereupon he beckoned to the young girl, and when she once more besought his permission to go, he left the room with the commanding cry, "You are to wait!"

He had rather far to go and some steps to mount in order to reach the balcony which ran round the base of the cupola of the Pantheon which his father had joined to the Serapeum, yet he undertook this willingly, as thence he could best be seen and heard.

A few hours earlier it would have been impossible for him to reach this point, and Epagathos had arranged that a sedan-chair and strong bearers should be waiting at the foot of the steps; but he refused it, for he felt entirely restored, and the shouts of his warriors intoxicated him like sparkling wine.

Meanwhile Melissa remained behind in the audience-chamber. She must obey Caesar's command. Yet it frightened her; and, besides, she was woman enough to feel it as an offense that the man who had assured her so sincerely of his gratitude, and who even feigned to love her, should have refused so harshly her desire to rest. She foresaw that, as long as he remained in Alexandria, she would have to be his constant companion. She trembled at the idea; yet, if she tried to fly from him, all she loved would be lost. No, this must not be thought of! She must remain.

She threw herself on a divan, lost in thought, and as she realized the confidence of which the unapproachable, proud emperor had thought her worthy, a secret voice whispered to her that it was certainly a delightful thing to share the overwhelming agitations of the highest and greatest. And was he then really bad, he who felt the necessity of vindicating himself before a simple girl, and to whom it appeared so intolerable to be misjudged and condemned even by her? Besides being the emperor and a suffering man, Caracalla had also become her wooer. It never once entered her mind to accept him; but still it flattered her extremely that the greatest of men should declare his love for her. Why, then, need she fear him? She was so important to him, she could do so much for him, that he would surely take care not to insult or offend her. This modest child, who till quite lately had trembled before her own father's temper, now, in the consciousness of Caesar's favor, felt herself strong to triumph over the wrath and passions of the most powerful and most terrible of men. In the mean time she dared not risk confessing to him that she was another's bride, for that might determine him to let Diodoros feel his power. The thought that the emperor could care about her good opinion greatly pleased her; it even had the effect of raising the hope in her inexperienced mind that Caracalla would moderate his passion for her sake—when old Adventus came into the room.

He was in a hurry; for preparations had to be made in the dining-hall for the reception of the ambassadors. But when at his appearance Melissa rose from the divan he begged her good-naturedly to continue resting. No one could tell what humor Caracalla might be in when he returned. She had often seen how rapidly that chameleon could change color. Who that had seen him just now, going to meet his soldiers, would believe that he had a few hours before sent away, with hard words, the widow of the Egyptian governor, who had come to beg mercy for her husband?

"So that wretch, Theocritus, has really carried out his intention of ruining the honest Titianus?" asked Melissa, horrified.

"Not only of ruining him," answered the chamberlain; "Titianus is by this time beheaded."

The old man bowed and left the room; but Melissa remained behind, feeling as if the floor had opened in front of her. He, whose ardent assurance she had just now believed, that he had been forced to shed the blood of an impious wretch, in obedience to an overpowering fate, was capable of allowing the noblest of men to be beheaded, unjudged, merely to please a mercenary favorite! His confession, then, had been nothing but a revolting piece of acting! He had endeavored to vanquish the disgust she felt for him merely to ensnare her and her healing hand more surely—as his plaything, his physic, his sleeping draught. And she had entered the trap, and acquitted him of the most horrible blood-guiltiness.

He had that very day rejected, without pity, a noble Roman lady who petitioned for her husband's life, and with the same breath he had afterwards befooled her!

She started up, indignant and deeply wounded. Was it not ignominious even to wait here like a prisoner in obedience to the command of this wretch? And she had dared for one moment to compare this monster with Diodoros, the handsomest, the best, and most amiable of youths!

It seemed to her inconceivable. If only he had not the power to destroy all that was dearest to her heart, what pleasure it would have been to shout in his face:

"I detest you, murderer, and I am the betrothed of another, who is as good and beautiful as you are vile and odious!"

Then the question occurred to her whether it was only for the sake of her healing hands that he had felt attracted to her, and had made her an avowal as if she were his equal.

The blood mounted to her face at this thought, and with a burning brow she walked to the open window.

A crowd of presentiments rushed into her innocent and, till then, unsuspecting heart, and they were all so alarming that it was a relief to her when a shout of joy from the panoplied breasts of several thousand armed men rent the air. Mingling with this overpowering demonstration of united rejoicing from such huge masses, came the blare of the trumpets and horns of the assembled legions. What a maddening noise!

Before her lay the square, filled with many legions of warriors who surrounded the Serapeum in their shining armor, with their eagles and vexilla. The praetorians stood by the picked men of the Macedonian phalanx, and with these were all the troops who had escorted the imperial general hither, and the garrisons of the city of Alexander who hoped to be called out in the next war.

On the balcony, decorated with statues which surrounded the colonnade of the Pantheon on which the cupola rested, she saw Caracalla, and at a respectful distance a superb escort of his friends, in red and white togas, bordered with purple stripes, and wearing armor. Having taken off his gold helmet, the imperial general bowed to his people, and at every nod of his head, and each more vigorous movement, the enthusiastic cheers were renewed more loudly than ever.

Macrinus then stepped up to Caesar's side, and the lictors who followed him, by lowering their fasces, signaled to the warriors to keep silence.

Instantly the ear-splitting din changed to a speechless lull.

At first she still heard the lances and shields, which several of the warriors had waved in enthusiastic joy, ringing against the ground, and the clatter of the swords being put back in their sheaths; then this also ceased, and finally, although only the superior officers had arrived on horseback, the stamping of hoofs, the snorting of the horses, and the rattle of the chains at their bits, were the only sounds.

Melissa listened breathlessly, looking first at the square and the soldiers below, then at the balcony where the emperor stood. In spite of the aversion she felt, her heart beat quicker. It was as if this immeasurable army had only one voice; as if an irresistible force drew all these thousands of eyes toward one point—the one little man up there on the Pantheon.

Directly he began to speak, Melissa's glance was also fixed on Caracalla.

She only heard the closing sentence, as, with raised voice, he shouted to the soldiers; and from it she gathered that he thanked his companions in arms for their anxiety, but that he still felt strong enough to share all their difficulties with them. Severe exertions lay behind them. The rest in this luxurious city would do them all good. There was still much to be conquered in the rich East, and to add to what they had already won, before they could return to Rome to celebrate a well-earned triumph. The weary should make themselves comfortable here. The wealthy merchants in whose houses he had quartered them had been told to attend to their wants, and if they neglected to do so every single warrior was man enough to show them what a soldier needed for his comfort. The people here looked askance at him and his soldiers, but too much moderation would be misplaced.

There certainly were some things even here which the host was not bound to supply to his military; he, Caesar, would provide them with these, and for that purpose he had put aside two million denarii out of his own poverty to distribute among them.

This speech had several times been interrupted by applause, but now such a tremendous shout of joy went up that it would have drowned the loudest thunder. The number of voices as well as their power seemed to have doubled.

Caracalla had added another link to the golden chain which already bound him to these faithful people; and, as he smiled and nodded to the delighted crowd from the balcony, he looked like a happy, light-hearted youth who had prepared a great treat for himself and several beloved friends.

What he said further was lost in the confusion of voices in the square. The ranks were broken up, and the cuirasses, helmets, and arms of the moving warriors caught the sun and sent bright beams of light crossing one another over the wide space surrounded with dazzling white marble statues.

When Caracalla left the balcony, Melissa drew back from the window.

The compassionate impulse to lighten the lot of a sufferer, which had before drawn her so strongly to Caracalla, had now lost its sense and meaning for this healthy, high-spirited man. She considered herself cheated, as if she had been fooled by sham suffering into giving excessively large alms to an artful beggar.

Besides, she loved her native town, and Caracalla's advice to the soldiers to force the citizens to provide luxurious living for them, had made her considerably more rebellious. If he ever put her again in a position to speak her mind freely to him, she would tell him all undisguisedly; but instantly it again rushed into her mind that she must keep guard over her tongue before the easily unchained wrath of this despot, until her father and brothers were in safety once more.

Before the emperor returned, the room was filled with people, of whom she knew none, excepting her old friend the white-haired, learned Samonicus. She was the aim and center of all eyes, and when even the kindly old man greeted her from a distance, and so contemptuously, that the blood rushed to her face, she begged Adventus to take her into the next room.

The Chamberlain did as she wished, but before he left her he whispered to her: "Innocence is trusting; but it is not of much avail here. Take care, child! They say there are sand-banks in the Nile which, like soft pillows, entice one to rest. But if you use them they become alive, and a crocodile creeps out, with open jaws. I am talking already in metaphor, like an Alexandrian, but you will understand me."

Melissa bowed acknowledgment to him, and the old man went on:

"He may perhaps forget you; for many things had accumulated during his illness. If the mass of business, as it comes in, is not settled for twenty four hours, it swells like a mill-stream that has the sluice down. But when work is begun, it quite carries him away. He forgets then to eat and drink. Ambassadors have arrived also from the Empress-mother, from Armenia, and Parthia. If he does not ask for you in half an hour, it will be suppertime, and I will let you out through that door."

"Do so at once," begged Melissa, with raised, petitioning hands; but the old man replied: "I should then reward you but ill for having warmed my feet for me. Remember the crocodile under the sand! Patience, child! There is Caesar's zithern. If you can play, amuse yourself with that. The door shuts closely and the curtains are thick. My old ears just now were listening to no purpose."

But Caracalla was so far from forgetting Melissa that although he had attended to the communication brought to him by the ambassadors, and the various dispatches from the senate, he asked for her even at the door of the tablinum. He had seen her from the balcony looking out on the square; so she had witnessed the reception his soldiers had given him. The magnificent spectacle must have impressed her and filled her with joy. He was anxious to hear all this from her own lips, before he settled down to work.

Adverntus whispered to him where he had taken her, to avoid the persecuting glances of the numerous strangers, and Caracalla nodded to him approvingly and went into the next room.

She sat there with the zithern, letting her fingers glide gently over the strings.

On his entering, she drew back hastily; but he cried to her brightly: "Do not disturb yourself. I love that instrument. I am having a statue erected to Mesomedes, the great zithern-player—you perhaps know his songs. This evening, when the feast and the press of work are over, I will hear how you play. I will also playa few airs to you."

Melissa then plucked up courage and said, decidedly: "No, my lord; I am about to bid you farewell for to-day."

"That sounds very determined," he answered, half surprised and half amused. "But may I be allowed to know what has made you decide on this step?"

"There is a great deal of work waiting for you," she replied, quietly.

"That is my affair, not yours," was the crushing answer.

"It is also mine," she said, endeavoring to keep calm; "for you have not yet completely recovered, and, should you require my help again this evening, I could not attend to your call."

"No?" he asked, wrathfully, and his eyelids began to twitch.

"No, my lord; for it would not be seemly in a maiden to visit you by night, unless you were ill and needed nursing. As it is, I shall meet your friends— my heart stands still only to think of it—"

"I will teach them what is due to you!" Caracalla bellowed out, and his brow was knit once more.

"But you can not compel me," she replied, firmly, "to change my mind as to what is seemly," and the courage which failed her if she met a spider, but which stood by her in serious danger as a faithful ally, made her perfectly steadfast as she eagerly added: "Not an hour since you promised me that so long as I remained with you I should need no other protector, and might count on your gratitude. But those were mere words, for, when I besought you to grant me some repose, you scorned my very reasonable request, and roughly ordered me to remain and attend on you."

At this Caesar laughed aloud.

"Just so! You are a woman, and like all the rest. You are sweet and gentle only so long as you have your own way."

"No, indeed," cried Melissa, and her eyes filled with tears. "I only look further than from one hour to the next. If I should sacrifice what I think right, merely to come and go at my own will, I should soon be not only miserable myself, but the object of your contempt."

Overcome by irresistible distress, she broke into loud sobs; but Caracalla, with a furious stamp of his foot, exclaimed:

"No tears! I can not, I will not see you weep. Can any harm come to you? Nothing but good; nothing but the best of happiness do I propose for you. By Apollo and Zeus, that is the truth! Till now you have been unlike other women, but when you behave like them, you shall—I swear it —you shall feel which of us two is the stronger!"

He roughly snatched her hand away from her face and thereby achieved his end, for her indignation at being thus touched by a man's brutal hand gave Melissa strength to suppress her sobs. Only her wet cheeks showed what a flood of tears she had shed, as, almost beside herself with anger, she exclaimed:

"Let my hand go! Shame on the man who insults a defenseless girl! You swear! Then I, too, may take an oath, and, by the head of my mother, you shall never see me again excepting as a corpse, if you ever attempt violence! You are Caesar—you are the stronger. Who ever doubted it? But you will never compel me to a vile action, not if you could inflict a thousand deaths on me instead of one!"

Caracalla, without a word, had released her hand and was staring at her in amazement.

A woman, and so gentle a woman, defying him as no man would have dared to do!

She stood before him, her hand raised, her bosom heaving; a flame of anger sparkled in her eyes through their tears, and he had never before thought her so fair. What majesty there was in this girl, whose simple grace had made him more than once address her as "child"! She was like a queen, an empress; perhaps she might become one. The idea struck him for the first time. And that little hand which now fell—what soothing power it had, how much he owed to it! How fervently he had wished but just now to be understood by her, and to be thought better of by her than by the rest! And this wish still possessed him. Nay, he was more strongly attracted than ever to this creature, worthy as she was of the highest in the land, and made doubly bewitching by her proud willfulness. That he should see her for the last time seemed to him as impossible as that he should never again see daylight; and yet her whole aspect announced that her threat was serious.

His aggrieved pride and offended sense of absolute power struggled with his love, repentance, and fear of losing her healing presence; but the struggle was brief, especially as a mass of business to be attended to lay before him like a steep hill to climb, and haste was imperative.

He went up to her, shaking his head, and said in the superior tone of a sage rebuking thoughtlessness:

"Like all the rest of them—I repeat it. My demands had no object in view but to make you happy and derive comfort from you. How hot must the blood be which boils and foams at the contact of a spark! Only too like my own; and, since I understand you, I find it easy to forgive you. Indeed, I must finally express myself grateful; for I was in danger of neglecting my duties as a sovereign for the sake of pleasing my heart. Go, then, and rest, while I devote myself to business."

At this, Melissa forced herself to smile, and said, still somewhat tearfully: "How grateful I am! And you will not again require me to remain, will you, when I assure you that it is not fitting?"

"Unluckily, I am not in the habit of yielding to a girl's whims."

"I have no whims," she eagerly declared. "But you will keep your word now, and allow me to withdraw? I implore you to let me go!"

With a deep sigh and an amount of self-control of which he would yesterday have thought himself incapable, he let go her hand, and she with a shudder thought that she had found the answer to the question he had asked her. His eyes, not his words, had betrayed it; for a woman can see in a suitor's look what color his wishes take, while a woman's eyes only tell her lover whether or no she reciprocates his feelings.

"I am going," she said, but he remarked the deadly paleness which overspread her features, and her colorless cheeks encouraged him in the belief that, after a sleepless night and the agitations of the last few hours, it was only physical exhaustion which made Melissa so suddenly anxious to escape from him. So, saying kindly:

"'Till to-morrow, then," he dismissed her.

But when she had almost left the room, he added: "One thing more! To-morrow we will try our zitherns together. After my bath is the time I like best for such pleasant things; Adventus will fetch you. I am curious to hear you play and sing. Of all sounds, that of the human voice is the sweetest. Even the shouting of my legions is pleasing to the ear and heart. Do you not think so, and does not the acclamation of so many thousands stir your soul?"

"Certainly," she replied hastily; and she longed to reproach him for the injustice he was doing the populace of Alexandria to benefit his warriors, but she felt that the time was ill chosen, and everything gave way to her longing to be gone out of the dreadful man's sight.

In the next room she met Philostratus, and begged him to conduct her to the lady Euryale; for all the anterooms were now thronged, and she had lost the calm confidence in which she had come thither.

CHAPTER XXII.

As Melissa made her way with the philosopher through the crowd, Philostratus said to her: "It is for your sake, child, that these hundreds have had so long to wait to-day, and many hopes will be disappointed. To satisfy all is a giant's task. But Caracalla must do it, well or ill."

"Then he will forget me!" replied Melissa, with a sigh of relief.

"Hardly," answered the philosopher. He was sorry for the terrified girl, and in his wish to lighten her woes as far as he could, he said, gravely: "You called him terrible, and he can be more terrible than any man living. But he has been kind to you so far, and, if you take my advice, you will always seem to expect nothing from him that is not good and noble."

"Then I must be a hypocrite," replied Melissa. "Only to-day he has murdered the noble Titianus."

"That is an affair of state which does not concern you," replied Philostratus. "Read my description of Achilles. I represent him among other heroes such as Caracalla might be. Try, on your part, to see him in that light. I know that it is sometimes a pleasure to him to justify the good opinion of others. Encourage your imagination to think the best of him. I shall tell him that you regard him as magnanimous and noble."

"No, no!" cried Melissa; "that would make everything worse."

But the philosopher interrupted her.

"Trust my riper experience. I know him. If you let him know your true opinion of him, I will answer for nothing. My Achilles reveals the good qualities with which he came into the world; and if you look closely you may still find sparks among the ashes."

He here took his leave, for they had reached the vestibule leading to the high-priest's lodgings, and a few minutes later Melissa found herself with Euryale, to whom she related all that she had seen and felt. When she told her older friend what Philostratus had advised, the lady stroked her hair, and said: "Try to follow the advice of so experienced a man. It can not be very difficult. When a woman's heart has once been attached to a man—and pity is one of the strongest of human ties—the bond may be strained and worn, but a few threads must always remain."

But Melissa hastily broke in:

"There is not a spider's thread left which binds me to that cruel man. The murder of Titianus has snapped them all."

"Not so," replied the lady, confidently. "Pity is the only form of love which even the worst crime can not eradicate from a kind heart. You prayed for Caesar before you knew him, and that was out of pure human charity. Exercise now a wider compassion, and reflect that Fate has called you to take care of a hapless creature raving in fever and hard to deal with. How many Christian women, especially such as call themselves deaconesses, voluntarily assume such duties! and good is good, right is right for all, whether they pray to one God or to several. If you keep your heart pure, and constantly think of the time which shall be fulfilled for each of us, to our ruin or to our salvation, you will pass unharmed through this great peril. I know it, I feel it."

"But you do not know him," exclaimed Melissa, "and how terrible he can be! And Diodoros! When he is well again, if he hears that I am with Caesar, in obedience to his call whenever he sends for me, and if evil tongues tell him dreadful things about me, he, too, will condemn me!"

"No, no," the matron declared, kissing her brow and eyes. "If he loves you truly, he will trust you."

"He loves me," sobbed Melissa; "but, even if he does not desert me when I am thus branded, his father will come between us."

"God forbid!" cried Euryale. "Remain what you are, and I will always be the same to you, come what may; and those who love you will not refuse to listen to an old woman who has grown gray in honor."

And Melissa believed her motherly, kind, worthy friend; and, with the new confidence which revived in her, her longing for her lover began to stir irresistibly. She wanted a fond glance from the eyes of the youth who loved her, and to whom, for another man's sake, she could not give all his due, nay, who had perhaps a right to complain of her. This she frankly confessed, and the matron herself conducted the impatient girl to see Diodoros.

Melissa again found Andreas in attendance on the sufferer, and she was surprised at the warmth with which the high-priest's wife greeted the Christian.

Diodoros was already able to be dressed and to sit up. He was pale and weak, and his head was still bound up, but he welcomed the girl affectionately, though with a mild reproach as to the rarity of her visits.

Andreas had already informed him that Melissa was kept away by her mediation for the prisoners, and so he was comforted by her assurance that if her duty would allow of it she would never leave him again. And the joy of having her there, the delight of gazing into her sweet, lovely face, and the youthful gift of forgetting the past in favor of the present, silenced every bitter reflection. He was soon blissfully listening to her with a fresh color in his cheeks, and never had he seen her so tender, so devoted, so anxious to show him the fullness of her great love. The quiet, reserved girl was to-day the wooer, and with the zeal called forth by her ardent wish to do him good, she expressed all the tenderness of her warm heart so frankly and gladly that to him it seemed as though Eros had never till now pierced her with the right shaft.

As soon as Euryale was absorbed in conversation with Andreas, she offered him her lips with gay audacity, as though in defiance of some stern dragon of virtue, and he, drunk with rapture, enjoyed what she granted him. And soon it was he who became daring, declaring that there would be time enough to talk another day; that for the present her rosy mouth had nothing to do but to cure him with kisses. And during this sweet give and take, she implored him with pathetic fervor never, never to doubt her love, whatever he might hear of her. Their older friends, who had turned their backs on the couple and were talking busily by a window, paid no heed to them, and the blissful conviction of being loved as ardently as she loved flooded her whole being.

Only now and then did the thought of Caesar trouble for a moment the rapture of that hour, like a hideous form appearing out of distant clouds. She felt prompted indeed to tell her lover everything, but it seemed so difficult to make him understand exactly how everything had happened, and Diodoros must not be distressed. And, indeed, intoxicated as he was with heated passion, he made the attempt impossible.

When he spoke it was only to assure her of his love; and when the lady Euryale at last called her to go, and looked in the girl's glowing face, Melissa felt as though she were snatched from a rapturous dream.

In the anteroom they were stopped by Andreas. Euryale had indeed relieved his worst fears, still he was anxious to lay before the girl the question whether she would not be wise to take advantage of this very night to make her escape. She, however, her eyes still beaming with happiness, laid her little hand coaxingly on his bearded mouth, and begged him not to sadden her high spirits and hopes of a better time by warnings and dismal forecasts. Even the lady Euryale had advised her to trust fearlessly to herself, and sitting with her lover she had acquired the certainty that it was best so. The freedman could not bear to disturb this happy confidence, and only impressed on Melissa that she should send for him if ever she needed him. He would find her a hiding- place, and the lady Euryale had undertaken to provide a messenger. He then bade them godspeed, and they returned to the high-priest's dwelling.

In the vestibule they found a servant from the lady Berenike; in his mistress's name he desired Euryale to send Melissa to spend the night with her.

This invitation, which would remove Melissa from the Serapeum, was welcome to them both, and the matron herself accompanied the young girl down a private staircase leading to a small side-door. Argutis, who had come to inquire for his young mistress, was to be her escort and to bring her back early next morning to the same entrance.

The old slave had much to tell her. He had been on his feet all day. He had been to the harbor to inquire as to the return of the vessel with the prisoners on board; to the Serapeum to inquire for her; to Dido, to give her the news. He had met Alexander in the forenoon on the quay where the imperial galleys were moored. When the young man learned that the trireme could not come in before next morning at the soonest, he had set out to cross the lake and see Zeus and his daughter. He had charged Argutis to let Melissa know that his longing for the fair Agatha gave him no peace.

He and old Dido disapproved of their young master's feather-brain, which had not been made more steady and patient even by the serious events of this day and his sister's peril; however, he did not allow a word of blame to escape him. He was happy only to be allowed to walk behind Melissa, and to hear from her own lips that all was well with her, and that Caesar was gracious.

Alexander, indeed, had also told the old man that he and Caesar were "good friends"; and now the slave was thinking of Pandion, Theocritus, and the other favorites of whom he had heard; and he assured Melissa that, as soon as her father should be free, Caracalla would be certain to raise him to the rank of knight, to give him lands and wealth, perhaps one of the imperial residences on the Bruchium. Then he, Argutis, would be house steward, and show that he knew other things besides keeping the workroom and garden in order, splitting wood, and buying cheaply at market.

Melissa laughed and said he should be no worse off if only the first wish of her heart were fulfilled, and she were wife to Diodoros; and Argutis declared he would be amply content if only she allowed him to remain with her.

But she only half listened and answered absently, for she breathed faster as she pictured to herself how she would show Caesar, on whom she had already proved her power, that she had ceased to tremble before him.

Thus they came to the house of Seleukus.

A large force had taken up their quarters there. In the pillared hall beyond the vestibule bearded soldiers were sitting on benches or squatting in groups on the ground, drinking noisily and singing, or laughing and squabbling as they threw the dice on the costly mosaic pavement. A riotous party were toping and reveling in the beautiful garden of the impluvium round a fire which they had lighted on the velvet turf. A dozen or so of officers had stretched themselves on cushions under one of the colonnades, and, without attempting to check the wild behavior of their men, were watching the dancing of some Egyptian girls who had been brought into the house of their involuntary host. Although Melissa was closely veiled and accompanied by a servant, she did not escape rude words and insolent glances. Indeed, an audacious young praetorian had put out his hand to pull away her veil, but an older officer stopped him.

The lady Berenike's rooms had so far not been intruded on; for Macrinus, the praetorian prefect, who knew Berenike through her brother-in-law the senator Coeranus, had given orders that the women's apartments were to be exempt from the encroachments of the quartermaster of the body-guard. Breathing rapidly and with a heightened color, Melissa at last entered the room of Seleukus's wife.

The matron's voice was full of bitterness as she greeted her young visitor with the exclamation "You look as if you had fled to escape persecution! And in my house, too! Or"—and her large eyes flashed brightly—"or is the blood-hound on the track of his prey? My boat is quite ready—" When Melissa denied this, and related what had happened, Berenike exclaimed: "But you know that the panther lies still and gathers himself up before he springs; or, if you do not, you may see it to-morrow at the Circus. There is to be a performance in Caesar's honor, the like of which not even Nero ever saw. My husband bears the chief part cf the cost, and can think of nothing else. He has even forgotten his only child, and all to please the man who insults us, robs and humiliates us! Now that men kiss the hands which maltreat them, it is the part of women to defy them. You must fly, child! The harbor is now closed, but it will be open again to-morrow morning, and, if your folks are set free in the course of the day, then away with you at once! Or do you really hope for any good from the tyrant who has made this house what you now see it?"

"I know him," replied Melissa, "and I look for nothing but the worst."

At this the elder woman warmly grasped the girl's hand, but she was interrupted by the waiting woman Johanna, who said that a Roman officer of rank, a tribune, craved to be admitted.

When Berenike refused to receive him, the maid assured her that he was a young man, and had expressed his wish to bring an urgent request to the lady's notice in a becoming and modest manner.

On this the matron allowed him to be shown in to her, and Melissa hastily obeyed her instructions to withdraw into the adjoining room.

Only a half-drawn curtain divided it from the room where Berenike received the soldier, and without listening she could hear the loud voice which riveted her attention as soon as she had recognized it.

The young tribune, in a tone of courteous entreaty, begged his hostess to provide a room for his brother, who was severely wounded. The sufferer was in a high fever, and the physician said that the noise and rattle of vehicles in the street, on which the room where he now lay looked out, and the perpetual coming and going of the men, might endanger his life. He had just been told that on the side of the women's apartments there was a row of rooms looking out on the impluvium, and he ventured to entreat her to spare one of them for the injured man. If she had a brother or a child, she would forgive the boldness of his request.

So far she listened in silence; then she suddenly raised her head and measured the petitioner's tall figure with a lurid fire in her eye. Then she replied, while she looked into his handsome young face with a half- scornful, half-indignant air: "Oh, yes! I know what it is to see one we love suffer. I had an only child; she was the joy of my heart. Death— death snatched her from me, and a few days later the sovereign whom you serve commanded us to prepare a feast for him. It seemed to him something new and delightful to hold a revel in a house of mourning. At the last moment—all the guests were assembled—he sent us word that he himself did not intend to appear. But his friends laughed and reveled wildly enough! They enjoyed themselves, and no doubt praised our cook and our wine. And now—another honor we can duly appreciate!— he sends his praetorians to turn this house of mourning into a tavern, a wine-shop, where they call creatures in from the street to dance and sing. The rank to which you have risen while yet so young shows that you are of good family, so you can imagine how highly we esteem the honor of seeing your men trampling, destroying, and burning in their camp-fires everything which years of labor and care had produced to make our little garden a thing of beauty. Only look down on them! Macrinus, who commands you, promised me, moreover, that the women's apartments should be respected. No praetorian, whether common soldier or commander,' and here she raised her voice, "shall set foot within them! Here is his writing. The prefect set the seal beneath it in Caesar's name."

"I know of the order, noble lady," interrupted Nemesianus, "and should be the last to wish to act against it. I do not demand, I only appeal humbly to the heart of a woman and a mother.'

"A mother!" broke in Berenike, scornfully; "yes! and one whose soul your lord has pierced with daggers—a woman whose home has been dishonored and made hateful to her. I have enjoyed sufficient honor now, and shall stand firmly on my rights."

"Hear but one thing more," began the youth, timidly; but the lady Berenike had already turned her back upon him, and returned with a proud and stately carriage to Melissa in the adjoining apartment.

Breathing hard, as if stunned by her words, the tribune remained standing on the threshold where the terrible lady had vanished from his sight, and then, striving to regain his composure, pushed back the curling locks from his brow. But scarcely had Berenike entered the other room than Melissa whispered to her: "The wounded man is the unfortunate Aurelius, whose face Caracalla wounded for my sake."

At this the lady's eyes suddenly flashed and blazed so strangely that the girl's blood ran cold. But she had no time to ask the reason of this emotion, for the next moment the queenly woman grasped the weaker one by the wrist with her strong right hand, and with a commanding "Come with me," drew her back into the room they had just quitted. She called to the tribune, whose hand was already on the door, to come back.

The young man stood still, surprised and startled to see Melissa; but the lady Berenike said, calmly, "Now that I have learned the honor that has been accorded to you, too, by the master whom you so faithfully serve, the poor injured man whom you call your brother shall be made welcome within these walls. He is my companion in suffering. A quiet, airy chamber shall be set apart for him, and he shall not lack careful attention, nor anything which even his own mother could offer him. Only two things I desire of you in return: that you admit no one of your companions-in-arms, nor any man whatever, into this dwelling, save only the physician whom I shall send to you. Furthermore, that you do not betray, even to your nearest friend, whom you found here besides myself."

Under the mortification that had wounded his brotherly heart, Aurelius Nemesianus had lost countenance; but now he replied with a soldier's ready presence of mind: "It is difficult for me to find a proper answer to you, noble lady. I know right well that I owe you my warmest thanks, and equally so that he whom you call our master has inflicted as deep a wrong on us as on you; but Caesar is still my military chief."

"Still!" broke in Berenike. "But you are too youthful a tribune for me to believe that you took up the sword as a means of livelihood."

"We are sons of the Aurelia," answered Nemesianus, haughtily, "and it is very possible that this day's work may be the cause of our deserting the eagles we have followed in order to win glory and taste the delights of warfare. But all that is for the future to decide. Meanwhile, I thank you, noble lady, and also in the name of my brother, who is my second self. On behalf of Apollinaris, too, I beg you to pardon the rudeness which we offered to this maiden—"

"I am not angry with you any more," cried Melissa, eagerly and frankly, and the tribune thanked her in his own and his brother's name.

He began trying to explain the unfortunate occurrence, but Berenike admonished him to lose no time. The soldier withdrew, and the lady Berenike ordered her handmaiden to call the housekeeper and other serving-women. Then she repaired quickly to the room she had destined for the wounded man and his brother. But neither Melissa nor the other women could succeed in really lending her any help, for she herself put forth all her cleverness and power of head and hand, forgetting nothing that might be useful or agreeable in the nursing of the sick. In that wealthy, well-ordered house everything stood ready to hand; and in less than a quarter of an hour the tribune Nemesianus was informed that the chamber was ready for the reception of his brother.

The lady then returned with Melissa to her own sleeping apartment, and took various little bottles and jars from a small medicine-chest, begging the girl at the same time to excuse her, as she intended to undertake the nursing of the wounded man herself. Here were books, and there Korinna's lute. Johanna would attend to the evening meal. Tomorrow morning they could consult further as to what was necessary to be done; then she kissed her guest and left the room.

Left to herself, Melissa gave herself up to varying thoughts, till Johanna brought her repast. While she hardly nibbled at it, the Christian told her that matters looked ill with the tribune, and that the wound in the forehead especially caused the physician much anxiety. Many questions were needed to draw this much from the freedwoman, for she spoke but little. When she did speak, however, it was with great kindliness, and there lay something so simple and gentle in her whole manner that it awakened confidence. Having satisfied her appetite, Melissa returned to the lady Berenike's apartment; but there her heart grew heavy at the thought of what awaited her on the morrow. When, at the moment of leaving, Johanna inquired whether she desired anything further, she asked her if she knew a saying of her fellow-believers, which ran, "The fullness of time was come."

"Yes, surely," returned the other; "our Lord himself spoke them, and Paul wrote them to the Galatians."

"Who is this Paul?" Melissa asked; and the Christian replied that of all the teachers of her faith he was the one she most dearly loved. Then, hesitating a little, she asked if Melissa, being a heathen, had inquired the meaning of this saying.

"Andrew, the freedman of Polybius and the lady Euryale, explained it to me. Did the moment ever come to you in which you felt assured that for you the time was fulfilled?"

"Yes," replied Johanna, with decision; "and that moment comes, sooner or later, in every life."

"You are a maiden like myself," began Melissa, simply. "A heavy task lies before me, and if you would confide to me—"

But the Christian broke in: "My life has moved in other paths than yours, and what has happened to me, the freedwoman and the Christian, can have no interest for you. But the saying which has stirred your soul refers to the coming of One who is all in all to us Christians. Did Andrew tell you nothing of His life?"

"Only a little," answered the girl, "but I would gladly hear more of Him."

Then the Christian seated herself at Melissa's side, and, clasping the maiden's hand in hers, told her of the birth of the Saviour, of His loving heart, and His willing death as a sacrifice for the sins of the whole world. The girl listened with attentive ear. With no word did she interrupt the narrative, and the image of the Crucified One rose before her mind's eye, pure and noble, and worthy of all love. A thousand questions rose to her lips, but, before she could ask one, the Christian was called away to attend the lady Berenike, and Melissa was again alone.

What she had already heard of the teaching of the Christians occurred to her once more, and above all that first saying from the sacred Scriptures which had attracted her attention, and about which she had just asked Johanna. Perhaps for her, too, the time was already fulfilled, when she had taken courage to defy the emperor's commands.

She rejoiced at this action, for she felt that the strength would never fail her now to set her will against his. She felt as though she bore a charm against his power since she had parted from her lover, and since the murder of the governor had opened her eyes to the true character of him on whom she had all too willingly expended her pity. And yet she shuddered at the thought of meeting the emperor again, and of having to show him that she felt safe with him because she trusted to his generosity.

Lost in deep thought, she waited for the return of the lady and the Christian waiting-woman, but in vain. At last her eye fell upon the scrolls which the lady Berenike had pointed out to her. They lay in beautiful alabaster caskets on an ebony stand. If they had only been the writings of the Christians, telling of the life and death of their Saviour! But how should writings such as those come here? The casket only held the works of Philostratus, and she took from it the roll containing the story of the hero of whom he had himself spoken to her. Full of curiosity, she smoothed out the papyrus with the ivory stick, and her attention was soon engaged by the lively conversation between the vintner and his Phoenician guest. She passed rapidly over the beginning, but soon reached the part of which Philostratus had told her. Under the form of Achilles he had striven to represent Caracalla as he appeared to the author's indulgent imagination. But it was no true portrait; it described the original at most as his mother would have wished him to be. There it was written that the vehemence flashing from the hero's bright eyes, even when peacefully inclined, showed how easily his wrath could break forth. But to those who loved him he was even more endearing during these outbursts than before. The Athenians felt toward him as they did toward a lion; for, if the king of beasts pleased them when he was at rest, he charmed them infinitely more when, foaming with bloodthirsty rage, he fell upon a bull, a wild boar, or some such ferocious animal.

Yes, indeed! Caracalla, too, fell mercilessly upon his prey! Had she not seen him hewing down Apollinaris a few hours ago?

Furthermore, Achilles was said to have declared that he could drive away care by fearlessly encountering the greatest dangers for the sake of his friends. But where were Caracalla's friends?

At best, the allusion could only refer to the Roman state, for whose sake the emperor certainly did endure many a hardship and many a wearisome task, and he was not the only person who had told her so.

Then she turned back a little and found the words: "But because he was easily inclined to anger, Chiron instructed him in music; for is it not inherent in this art to soothe violence and wrath—And Achilles acquired without trouble the laws of harmony and sang to the lyre."

This all corresponded with the truth, and tomorrow she was to discover what had suggested to Philostratus the story that when Achilles begged Calliope to endow him with the gifts of music and poetry she had given him so much of both as he required to enliven the feast and banish sadness. He was also said to be a poet, and devoted himself most ardently to verse when resting from the toils of war.

To hear that man unjustly blamed on whom her heart is set, only increases a woman's love; but unmerited praise makes her criticise him more sharply, and is apt to transform a fond smile into a scornful one. Thus the picture that raised Caracalla to the level of an Achilles made Melissa shrug her shoulders over the man she dreaded; and while she even doubted Caesar's musical capacities, Diodoros's young, fresh, bell-like voice rose doubly beautiful and true upon her memory's ear. The image of her lover finally drove out that of the emperor, and, while she seemed to hear the wedding song which the youths and maidens were so soon to sing for them both, she fell asleep.

It was late when Johanna came to admonish her to retire to rest. Shortly before sunrise she was awakened by Berenike, who wished to take some rest, and who told her, before seeking her couch, that Apollinaris was doing well. The lady was still sleeping when Johanna came to inform Melissa that the slave Argutis was waiting to see her.

The Christian undertook to convey the maiden's farewell greetings to her mistress.

As they entered the living-room, the gardener had just brought in fresh flowers, among them three rose-bushes covered with full-blown flowers and half-opened, dewy buds. Melissa asked Johanna timidly if the lady Berenike would permit her to pluck one—there were so many; to which the Christian replied that it would depend on the use it was to be put to.

"Only for the sick tribune," answered Melissa, reddening. So Johanna plucked two of the fairest blooms and gave them to the maiden—one for the man who had injured her and one for her betrothed. Melissa kissed her, gratefully, and begged her to present the flowers to the sick man in her name.

Johanna carried out her wish at once; but the wounded man, gazing mournfully at the rose, murmured to himself: "Poor, lovely, gentle child! She will be ruined or dead before Caracalla leaves Alexandria!"

Milton Keynes UK
Ingram Content Group UK Ltd.
UKHW010627080324
438959UK00005B/360

9 789357 947800